CHAPTER 85: TEARS

FINE! SUIT YOUR-SELF!

JUST KEEP SULKING FOR THE REST OF YOUR LIFE!!

CHAPTER 85: TEARS

I ONLY HOPE YOU'LL LIKE IT.

MERLA PUT A LOT OF WORK INTO IT!

FEEL UP TO SOME SUPPER, DARREN?

DAD!

STOP THAT, URCHA!

SHOW US HOW YOU DRINK BLOOD, DARREN!

CHIRU (SLURP)

"THANKS, LILIA..."

BUT MOMMY'S PASTA IS THE BEST!

NO... NOT HUNGRY.

THANKS, THOUGH, EVRA...

WELL, MAYBE NEXT TIME.

LET'S GO, SHAN-CUS.

EVERY-ONE'S GOT A RIGHT TO LEAN ON THEIR FRIENDS WHEN TIMES ARE HARD.

HE'S REALLY WORRIED ABOUT YOU, DARREN.

DON'T BE TOO HARD ON HARKAT, WILL YOU?

...MR. CREPS-LEY...?

WHAT AM I SUPPOSED TO DO NOW...

"THE REAL LORD OF THE VAM-PANEZE IS ME."

STEVE'S SHOCKING ADMISSION STILL RANG IN MY EARS.

WE LEFT MR. CREPSLEY'S CHARRED BONES IN THE PIT WHERE HE'D FALLEN...

THE WAR OF THE SCARS ISN'T OVER.

WE TRUDGED UP TO THE SURFACE, DRAGGING OUR WOUNDED HEARTS AND BODIES THROUGH THE SEWERS...

MR. CREPSLEY HAD DIED FOR NOTHING.

WE WALKED THROUGH THE HALLS, SHEDDING TEARS AS WE MOURNED HIS DEATH. ONLY I FOUND MYSELF UNABLE TO CRY...

AS MUCH AS I WANTED TO HOWL AND SOB WITH GRIEF, MY EYES REMAINED DRY AND STEELY.

WHO'S THERE?

I AM HERE TO HELP, NOT HARM...

PEACE, VANCHA.

WE'LL PUT EVERYTHING WE'VE GOT INTO THE FINAL CHANCE! I'LL FLIT FOR VAMPIRE MOUNTAIN AS SOON AS NIGHT FALLS.

AND WHERE DO YOU GO NOW?

THAT LEFT ONLY ONE MORE CHANCE...

I DON'T WANT TO RETURN FOR A WHILE. I'VE HAD ALL I CAN TAKE OF VAMPIRES AND VAMPANEZE...

WE KNOW THAT STEVE IS THEIR LORD NOW.

I'LL SET EVERY-ONE SEARCH-ING FOR HIM.

BUT HARKAT SAID THAT HE WOULD STAY WITH ME...

NO...

DARREN— ARE YOU AND HARKAT COMING?

IF YOU DON'T KNOW WHERE ELSE TO GO, DARREN... YOU CAN STAY WITH ME.

DEBBIE AND ALICE WOULD RETURN TO THEIR NORMAL LIVES...

YOU TWO CAN PRETEND THIS NEVER HAP-PENED. IF YOU DO, THE VAMPANEZE WON'T COME AGAIN.

......

HOLD ON TO THESE ...

KASA (RUSTLED)

IF HE DOESN'T, YOU CAN ALWAYS GO LOOKING FOR HIM.

WILL YOU EVER... COME BACK?

SOB

WHEN THE TWO OF YOU DECIDE UPON YOUR COURSE, OPEN THEM.

KEEP THEM CLOSED.

SO, SHALL WE BE GOING?

YOU'LL ESCORT A LADY, I PRESUME.

GOING ...?

WHERE ?

ZAAAA
(ZSHHH)

WAH
HA!
HA
HA!

ARE YOU IN HERE, DAR-REN?

I GOT SOME-THING FOR YOU.

TRUSKA...

FEEL LIKE SOME CAKE?

OH! SORRY, TRUSKA ...

BA (SNATCH)

WHAT ARE THESE? SUN-GLASS-ES?

BECHA (SPLAT)

LEAVE ME ALONE —

HUH...? I'M FINE!

GUI (TUG)

LET ME HELP CLEAN YOU UP.

THAT WHAT YOU GET FOR BEING BIG MOODY-GUTS!

HEE HEE!

HEY! WHAT THE HELL!?

YOU IS DIRTY AND SMELLY.

YOU DON'T KNOW WHAT I'M FEELING. NOBODY DOES!

YOU DON'T KNOW ANYTHING ABOUT IT.

...BUT YOU CAN'T SIT 'ROUND LIKE GRUMPY BEAR ALL TIME.

I KNOW YOU SAD, DARREN...

I HAD HUSBAND AND DAUGHTER.

THEY GET KILLED BY EVIL FISHERMEN.

FFII

ZAPA (SPLASH)

...TO LOSE SOMEBODY CLOSE?

YOU THINK YOU THE ONLY ONE...

MY DAUGHTER WAS LESS THAN TWO YEARS OLD WHEN SHE DIE.

I HURTED TERRIBLE INSIDE AND HAD TO GET AWAY.

THAT WHY I LEFT HOME AND JOINED WITH CIRQUE DU FREAK...

I DON'T TELL ANYONE HERE ABOUT IT YET...

WHA...?

WORST THING IS LETTING IT HURT YOU SO MUCH THAT YOU DIE TOO, INSIDE.

THE DEATH OF SOMEBODY YOU LOVE IS THE SECOND WORST THING IN WORLD...

IT HARD TO LIVE WITH SADNESS IF YOU CAN'T GET IT OUT WITH TEARS...

YOU WOULD BE DEAD...

...EVEN THOUGH YOUR BODY LIVES...

I LEAVE YOUR CLOTHES HERE.

DABO
(PLOP)

ゲ゛ボ゛"

LOOK INTO THE MIRROR...

YOU NOT FINISHED. HERE...

IT STILL A BIT TOO BIG FOR YOU.

I LOOK LIKE A CHILD...

READY?

LOOK DEEP IN THEM, AND DON'T TURN AWAY UNTIL YOU SEE...

LOOK AT YOUR EYES.

WAIT!

BA (SNATCH)

THEY LARTEN'S OLD CLOTHES. I'M GLAD WE STILL HAVE ONE OUTFIT IN WARDROBE.

ARE THESE ...?

IT ONLY NATURAL FOR A FATHER TO CARE FOR HIS SON.

NOT MR. CREPS-LEY!!

I WAS SUPPOSED TO BE IN THAT FIGHT!

WHAT WOULD HE SAY IF HE SAW THIS ALIVE-BUT-DEAD GAZE THAT WILL GET WORSE IF YOU NOT STOP?

LARTEN NOT WANT THIS. HE LOVE LIFE. HE WANT YOU TO LOVE IT TOO.

JUST LIKE A FATHER WITH NEWBORN CHILD...

LARTEN WAS VERY STRANGE WHEN YOU FIRST JOIN CIRQUE DU FREAK.

FA... THER ...?

...IN RE-
SPONSE
TO HIM?

AND
WHAT
YOU
SAY...

BUT...
MR.
CREPSLEY
SAID...

...HE WAS
SORRY...
FOR
MAKING
ME A
VAMPIRE
...

NOT A
WORD...

I COULDN'T
SAY ANY-
THING...

HERE...
IN YOUR
HEART.

LARTEN
IS LIS-
TENING
...

THEN
YOU
SAY IT
NOW.

TON
(TAP)

HE IS
ALWAYS...
AT YOUR
SIDE.

THE CIRQUE DU FREAK WAS BUSY PER-FORMING IN A LARGE TOWN ON THE COAST.

IT WAS THE THIRD STOP SINCE HARKAT AND I HAD RE-JOINED.

DARREN, TAKE THIS STUFF OVER TO TRUSKA'S TENT!

I'M ON IT!!

CHAPTER 86: DEPARTURE

THANKS.

HERE'S THE MATERIAL YOU WANTED.

IT FINALLY DONE, DARREN. COME LOOK!

HUH?

WE HAD QUITE AN AUDIENCE LAST NIGHT. GUESS THAT'S THE BENEFIT OF PLAYING SUCH A BIG CITY.

GARA (CLUNK)

GARA

CHAPTER 86:
DEPARTURE

...WHEN YOU BECOME GREAT VAMPIRE ...

WAITING FOR DAY YOU BECOME STRONG ENOUGH TO SUIT IT...

I TAKE VERY GOOD CARE OF IT.

WOW!

IT WAS VERY DAMAGED, SO TOOK A LONG TIME TO FIX...

I'M SURE MR. CREPS-LEY IS HAPPY.

THANK YOU, TRUS-KA!

MORNING, DARREN!

MORNING

IN THE MONTHS AFTER I'D FIRST CRIED IN TRUSKA'S TENT...

...I'D WEPT A LOT FOR MR. CREPSLEY.

ZUZU (SNIFF)

....

GRADUALLY THE TEARFUL BURSTS HAD LESSENED AS I CAME TO TERMS WITH MY LOSS AND LEARNED TO LIVE WITH IT.

IT HAD BEEN HORRIBLE, BUT NECESSARY.

FURA (SWISH)

FURA

FURA

IT'S GOOD TO HAVE THE SUPPORT OF SO MANY FRIENDS...

I'M SO GLAD I CAME BACK TO THE CIRQUE.

YOU LOOK AWFUL.

WHAT'S THE MATTER, HARKAT?

FUI (SPIN)

FURA

FURA (SWISH)

HE HAD TRIED HIS HARDEST TO CONSOLE ME WHEN MY GRIEF WAS DEEPEST, AND I HAD IGNORED HIS EFFORTS.

THINGS HAVE BEEN AWKWARD BETWEEN ME AND HARKAT.

FUUU (SIGH)

WE'RE SLEEP-ING IN SEPARATE TENTS.

NOW HE WON'T SPEAK TO ME AT ALL, EVEN WHEN I ATTEMPT TO REACH OUT TO HIM.

VISI-TORS? SURE, I GUESS ...

MAY I BRING THEM INTO YOUR TENT?

I HATE TO DISTURB YOU, BUT YOU HAVE VISITORS.

HOW CAN I MAKE IT UP TO HARKAT?

SFX: GORO (ROLL)

EXCEL-LENT.

MR. TALL!!

HELLO, DAR-REN.

COME IN.

AND ALICE! WHAT ARE YOU DOING HERE!?

DEBBIE!?

DARREN!!

(GABA HUG)

IT'S A LONG STORY...

THEY TOLD ME ALL ABOUT WHAT HAD HAPPENED SINCE WE PARTED.

WHAT!? YOU BOTH QUIT YOUR JOBS!?

I TRIED TO RETURN TO MY NORMAL LIFE, BUT EVERY TIME I THOUGHT OF WHAT HAPPENED DOWN THERE...

AND IF THE VAMPANEZE WIN THE WAR...

...IT DOESN'T SEEM LIKELY THAT THE VAMPETS WILL WANT TO STOP FIGHTING. THEY'LL TURN ON HUMANS NEXT.

...BUT NEITHER OF US KNOWS WHERE TO FIND THE PLACE!

WE WANTED TO TAKE THIS PLAN TO VAMPIRE MOUNTAIN FOR APPROVAL...

THOSE WHO DON'T WANT TO BE VICTIMS FIGHT FOR THEM-SELVES.

...TO FIGHT THE VAMPETS NOW, BEFORE THEY GROW TOO STRONG.

I SAID WE NEEDED TO RECRUIT HUMANS...

REMEMBER THE LETTERS THAT EVANNA GAVE US?

BUT HOW DID YOU KNOW WHERE TO FIND THE CIRQUE?

I'M NOT SURE HOW SHE KNEW WHERE IT WOULD BE, BUT I'LL TRY NOT TO THINK TOO HARD ABOUT IT.

I SEE. A MAP OF WHERE TO FIND THE CIRQUE...

LOOKS LIKE IT!

...I'M MEANT TO GUIDE YOU TO VAMPIRE MOUNTAIN?

I SUPPOSE THIS MEANS...

AND WHAT ABOUT HER? IS SHE HERE WITH YOU?

NOT ANYMORE. SHE WANDERED OFF A WHILE BACK.

I'M NOT EAGER TO GO BACK. IT'S STILL TOO SOON.

BUT FOR SOMETHING THIS IMPORTANT, I GUESS I DON'T HAVE MUCH OF A CHOICE.

UNLESS YOU HAVE OTHER PLANS?

HE'LL BE SO HAPPY TO SEE YOU AGAIN!

BASA (FLAP)

LET ME GO CALL HARKAT!

DEBBIE AND ALICE ARE HERE! WE'RE GOING BACK TO VAMPIRE M—

GOOD TIMING!

I'M AFRAID HE'S NOT GOING ANYWHERE WITH YOU...

KACHI (TICK)

KACHI

HARKAT!

HARKAT MUST LEAVE ON A JOURNEY TO DISCOVER HIS PAST... HIS IDENTITY.

IT WAS TOO BAD, WHAT HAPPENED TO LARTEN... BUT YOU SEEM TO BE DOING FINE NOW.

I SEE YOU SURVIVED YOUR RUN-IN WITH MASTER LEONARD.

WHY, HELLO! BEAUTIFUL LADIES!

DARREN?

MR. TINY...

......

DON'T DO IT. HARKAT IS A CLOSE FRIEND OF MINE.

IS THERE A PROBLEM?

WHAT DO YOU MEAN, "JOURNEY"?

ARE YOU GOING TO TAKE HARKAT WITH YOU?

YOU DON'T EVEN KNOW WHAT HARKAT'S GOING THROUGH, DO YOU?

HA-HA-HA... NOT A VERY ATTENTIVE FRIEND, ARE YOU?

...TRYING TO HIDE HIS PAIN FROM YOU...

OH, THE DEAR, CARING FRIEND...

...THE AGONY AS HE STRUGGLES BENEATH HIS CONSTRICTING ROBE, SCREAMING OUT IN THE MIDDLE OF THE NIGHT?

OF THE NIGHTMARES THAT PLAGUE HIM...

CAN YOU HAVE ANY IDEA, MASTER SHAN?

IS... IS THIS TRUE?

HARKAT...?

...YOUR CHANCES OF SURVIVAL ARE FAIR.

IF DARREN ACCOMPANIES YOU...

IT'S A ROAD THAT HE MUST TREAD...

ALONE, IT'S PRACTICALLY CERTAIN YOU'LL FAIL.

...UNLESS HE'D RATHER GO LOOPY AND DIE.

...ASSUMING YOU VALUE YOUR LIFE.

IN FACT, HARKAT, I THINK YOUNG SHAN SHOULD ACCOMPANY YOU...

THIS IS MY QUEST, NOT HIS.

DARREN'S NOT COMING. HE HAS PROBLEMS OF HIS OWN... WITH THE VAMPANEZE.

SAY IT, HARKAT!

HARKAT, MAYBE WE SHOULD ...

SAY YOU WANT ME TO BE WITH YOU...

DARREN GOES WITH DEBBIE AND... ALICE. END OF STORY!

OH? BUT ...

WELL, THERE YOU HAVE IT.

IT'S TIME YOU RETURNED TO THE FOLD.

NO. YOUR LOYALTY LIES WITH THE VAMPIRES.

I'LL BE FINE ON MY OWN.

AND A LITTLE SCARY!

GASA (RUSTLE)

ド"サ ド"サ

GASA

THIS IS SO EXCITING— OFF TO SEE VAMPIRE MOUNTAIN!!

DEBBIE TOLD ME IT WAS VERY IMPORTANT TO YOU.

ALICE SNUCK IT OUT OF THE PILE OF EVIDENCE THE POLICE COLLECTED!

......

OH, DARREN. THIS IS YOURS!

...MY DIARY!

THIS LOOKS LIKE...

DEBBIE, ALICE, THANK YOU!

AH... I SEE.

AH YES, THE TIME WHEN WE WERE ATTACKED BY THE BEAR THAT HAD DRUNK VAMPANEZE BLOOD...

IT'S FROM WHEN I FIRST WENT TO VAMPIRE MOUNTAIN.

PARA (FLIP)

...HE WAS AT MY SIDE...

WHENEVER I WAS IN TROUBLE...

HARKAT...

...YOU WOULD SAY THAT...

I HAD A FEELING...

I CAN'T GO WITH YOU...

I'M SORRY, DEBBIE. I JUST CAN'T...

DEB-BIE...

YOU SHOULD GO, DARREN.

BUT YOU'RE THE ONLY ONE WHO CAN HELP HIM NOW.

HA HA...

I'M TER-RIBLE, AREN'T I?

JUST TELL US THE WAY TO VAMPIRE MOUNTAIN. WE'LL TAKE CARE OF THE REST...

WHEN HARKAT TOLD YOU NOT TO GO WITH HIM, I FELT RELIEVED FOR A MOMENT...

DA (DASH)

HARKAT!!

JIWA (DRIP)

I'VE WAITED THIRTEEN YEARS AL-READY...

YOU'RE REALLY GOING TO LET HIM GO?

...I HOPE...

I'M SURE I'LL SEE HIM AGAIN...

I TOLD YOU NOT TO COME!

DARREN? WHY ARE YOU HERE!?

HAA

HAA (HUFF)

DAR-REN, YOU FOOL...

LET ME HANDLE SOME OF THE LOAD FOR ONCE.

YOU GOODY-TWO-SHOES! STOP WORRYING ABOUT ME...

...AND STOP TRYING TO HANDLE EVERY-THING ON YOUR OWN.

AH, MASTER SHAN! I THOUGHT YOU MIGHT SHOW UP!

AN-
OTHER
PLACE
...

AN-
OTHER
WORLD
...

WHERE
DOES
THIS
LEAD?

THIS IS THE
ONLY PATH
THAT WILL
TAKE YOU TO
HARKAT'S
TRUE
IDENTITY
...

A RED
DOOR-
WAY...

IS YOUR
SHORT,
GRAY-
SKINNED
FRIEND
WORTH
SUCH AN
ENORMOUS
RISK?

IF YOU GO WITH
HARKAT AND DIE,
YOU WON'T BE
HERE TO FACE
STEVE LEONARD
WHEN THE TIME
COMES, WITH
TERRIBLE
REPERCUSSIONS
FOR VAMPIRES
EVERYWHERE.

THINK
SERI-
OUSLY
ABOUT
THIS.

VERY
WELL.

YES
!!

TOPU
(SPLISH)

PROCEED,
THEN...

WHERE
...?

...HAVE
YOU EVER
FOUGHT A
PANTHER?

BY THE
WAY,
MASTER
SHAN...

CHAPTER 87: THE PIT

YOU WOULD STAND NO CHANCE IN A ONE-ON-ONE CONFRONTATION. YOU MUST POOL YOUR STRENGTH AND FORM A PLAN.

THE PANTHER IS ONE OF THE FIERCEST KILLERS IN NATURE.

...YOU WILL DISCOVER THE PATH YOU ARE MEANT TO TRAVEL...

GASA
(RUSTLE)

IF YOU CAN DEFEAT THE PANTHER THAT LURKS IN THE JUNGLE TO THE WEST...

GUEKUE
(BAWWK)

...TO THE LAKE OF SOULS!!

GURURURURURU
(GRRRRLL)

PIKU (TWITCH)

GUEE (GWAHH)

GUEE

HERE IT COMES!

IT'S A BIG ONE!

SUEUSU (SSSH)

GURURU (GRRR)

LET'S GET FARTHER AWAY. IT MUST HAVE SMELLED US...

YOU THINK IT NOTICED SOMETHING WAS WRONG...?

YOU SURE IT'S A PANTHER? NOT A SABER-TOOTHED TIGER?

THERE IT GOES...

GUE

GUE

I KNOW, BUT WE HAVE NO CHOICE... IF WE STAY HERE, IT'LL ALSO KNOW WHEN...IT RETURNS.

WE WON'T HAVE A CLEAR VIEW IF WE WITHDRAW ANY FARTHER.

GASA

GASA (RUSTLE)

THIS IS YOUR LIFE ON THE LINE! WE CAN'T AFFORD TO WAIT!

HOW CAN WE BE PATIENT!?

HOW ARE WE SUPPOSED TO BEAT THIS MONSTER WITH A SINGLE KNIFE?

THAT'S WHY WE DUG THAT PIT WITH THE...DEER HANGING OVER IT AS BAIT.

LET'S HAVE PATIENCE...

...

...

NO USE IN DOUBTING IT NOW. MR. TINY LEFT US HERE...AND THE ONLY CLUE WE HAVE TO RETURN TO OUR WORLD IS TO FIND THIS...LAKE OF SOULS.

WILL THE NIGHTMARES STOP?

SO WILL WE REALLY DISCOVER YOUR PAST LIFE IF WE FIND THIS "LAKE OF SOULS"?

STOP IT.

NOT AS TOUGH AS YOU, DARREN. YOU CAME ALONG.

HA-HA... YOU'RE ONE TOUGH CUSTOMER, HARKAT.

IF I WERE IN YOUR SPOT, I COULDN'T BE SO CALM AND COLLECTED.

PU
(PFFT)

NIGO
(SMIRK)

OH WELL, TOO LATE FOR THAT...

IF ONLY I WERE ACTUALLY ON MY WAY TO VAMPIRE MOUNTAIN WITH DEBBIE!

EVEN THEN... I'M GLAD YOU'RE HERE.

VUVUVU
(VMMM)

UGH.

THE PANTHER, DEER, INSECTS, PLANTS... THEY'RE ALL DIFFERENT FROM THE ONES WE KNOW...

I WONDER WHERE THE HELL WE ARE...

WAS THAT THE PANTHER'S ROAR!?

MAYBE IT FELL IN THE TRAP! LET'S GO!!

GUOOOOO
(ROAAAR)

MAYBE A FAR-OFF WORLD IN OUR OWN UNIVERSE!

IN A PAST VERSION OF EARTH? A PARALLEL DIMENSION?

WE PUT THOSE... STAKES IN THERE, DIDN'T WE? THE PIT...

DARREN?

...

NO SIGN OF THE DEER... MAYBE IT FELL IN WITH THE PANTHER?

I'D RATHER NOT LOOK... IF I CAN AVOID IT...

BURU (SHIVER)

BURU

I CAN SMELL BLOOD COMING FROM THE HOLE...

(SKFF)

SORRY, HARKAT...

GOOD POINT... I DON'T THINK YOU SHOULD LOOK...

WAIT
...

MAYBE
THE ROPE
HOLDING
THE
DEER...
JUST
SNAPPED.

BUT WE
JUST
HEARD
ITS
ROAR...

THERE'S
NO PAN-
THER...
JUST THE
DEER.

ITS
THROAT'S
BEEN
RIPPED
OPEN...

NO...

THE
PANTHER
MUST
BE...

GAAAA (GRAAH)

DOSHA (DSHH)

HARKAT!!!

HAA (HUFF)

HAA

HARKAT, NO!

NO...

HURRY AND... HELP ME UP.

WAIT! LOOK AT THIS...

MR. TINY SAID THAT WE WOULD KNOW WHERE...TO GO NEXT IF WE BEAT THE PANTHER.

I'M AMAZED WE OVER-CAME SUCH A MONSTER.

BUT LOOK AT THE SIZE OF THIS THING...

VAMPIRE EYE-SIGHT, MY FRIEND!

LETTERS? HOW DID YOU SEE THAT?

WOW, HARKAT... DON'T GET YOUR HANDS TOO DIRTY...

BOKI (CRUNCH)

MEKIKI (CRIIKK)

BAKI (CRACK)

OKAY! LET'S PULL THEM ALL OUT!

BUT... THAT SAYS...

WHAT!?

I HAVE A FEELING...

HAVE YOU WORKED IT OUT?

KACHA (CLICK)

WE MUST BE ABLE TO MAKE A MESSAGE OUT OF THESE.

......

WHAT COULD IT BE? "ASK... MUD"...?

HARKAT...

...MULDS.

THEY'RE HOLLOW ON THE INSIDE...

THESE TEETH ARE STRANGE.

HYUU (CWSHH)

MR. TINY LOVES PLAYING WITH TIME...

BA (SMACK)

IT'S NO HINT AT ALL, JUST A WASTE OF TIME!

AS I SUSPECTED... ANOTHER ONE OF MR. TINY'S JAPES.

WHAT KIND OF JOKE IS THIS?

WELL, THEY'RE SHARP... COULD BE USEFUL FOR SOMETHING.

GOSO (CRUSTLE)

YOU'RE TAKING THEM WITH YOU? WHAT FOR?

WHAT? REALLY!?

MAYBE WE SHOULD CUT ITS STOMACH OPEN...

......

DAMN YOU, MR. TINY! WHERE'S THE STUPID HINT!?

GASHI

GASHI (RUB)

GU CHRRG!

UGH...

ZO (SCRAPE)

ZO

ZO

WAIT, HAR-KAT!

THERE'S SOMETHING DRAWN ON THE SKIN...

GIVE ME THE KNIFE!

"GO TO THE...

HANG ON...

WHAT DOES IT SAY?

IT'S... A MAP. AND A MESSAGE...

"GRAB THE GELATI-NOUS... GLOBES..."

"...GO TO THE HOME OF THE WORLD'S LARGEST TOAD.

ACCORDING TO THE MAP, THIS SWAMP SHOULD BE WHERE WE'LL FIND THE TOAD...

ZUBU (SLURP)

A MONTH SINCE WE LEFT THE PANTHER'S JUNGLE... AND WE'RE FINALLY HERE.

IT COULD TAKE US MONTHS TO FIND THIS GIANT TOAD...

JITO (WIPE)

MR. TINY WANTS US TO FIND THE TOAD, SO I'M SURE HE'S FIDDLED WITH LAWS IN ORDER TO MAKE IT HAPPEN.

I WOULDN'T WORRY ABOUT THAT.

...TO SAY NOTHING OF THE GLOBES.

CHAPTER 88: GIANT TOAD

BUBAAAAA! (CROAAAK)

WHO KNOWS? MAYBE WE'LL HEAR ITS CROAK FROM HERE...

I DON'T THINK SO. MR. TINY'S SET THIS UP, BUT WE HAVE TO SWEAT TO MAKE IT HAPPEN.

BUT WE CAN'T JUST... WAIT FOR THE TOAD TO... COME TO US, RIGHT?

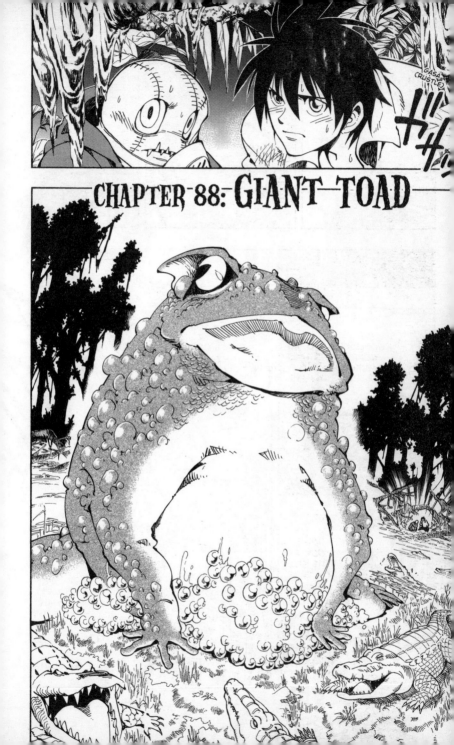

CHAPTER 88: GIANT TOAD

LOOK AT THE TOAD'S FEET, DARREN!

HE'LL SWALLOW US BOTH IN ONE GULP...

UGH... LOOK AT THE SIZE OF THAT BEAST!

THOSE MUST BE THE GELATINOUS GLOBES.

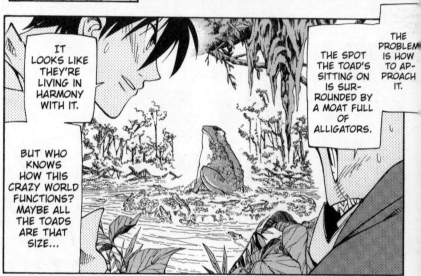

IT LOOKS LIKE THEY'RE LIVING IN HARMONY WITH IT.

BUT WHO KNOWS HOW THIS CRAZY WORLD FUNCTIONS? MAYBE ALL THE TOADS ARE THAT SIZE...

THE SPOT THE TOAD'S SITTING ON IS SURROUNDED BY A MOAT FULL OF ALLIGATORS.

THE PROBLEM IS HOW TO APPROACH IT.

ALL READY?

WELL, DARREN?

OKAY.

BUT WE NEED TO COLLECT SOME THINGS FIRST.

I'VE GOT A PLAN, HARKAT.

POTO
(SPLAT)

GAT
(GRAB)

BUN
(WHOOSH)

GA
(CHOMP)

GABU
(CHOMP)

JUST MAKE
SURE YOU
KEEP THOSE
GATORS
OCCUPIED!

HARKAT,
YOU TOSS
SOME BAIT
UP ONTO THE
ISLAND.

ZAPA
(SPLISH)

SUUU
(SHHH)

THAT'S IT,
HARKAT
...

JIII
(STARE)

BUN! (SLURP)

SOOOO (SNEAK)

UGH... IT'S ALL SQUISHY AND SLIMY...

SASASA (SWISH)

DON'T SCARE ME, YOU BIG UGLY BRUTE!

MUNYA (YAWN)

MUNYA (YAWN)

BUOOOO (BRRRUP)

THERE, THAT SHOULD BE ENOUGH!

NOW RUN FOR IT!!!

DA (DASH)

BASHA (SPLOSH)

AAGH!

BACHIN (SMACK)

DARREN!!

PIKU (TWITCH)

BWA

DARREN, GET ONTO DRY LAND!!

ZABA (SPLASH)

ZABA

THE ALLI-GATORS!!

ZABABA (SPLOSH)

...EVEN BY MY STANDARDS.

THAT WAS CUTTING IT PRETTY CLOSE...

ZUCHA (SPLOTCH)

BACHI (ZAP)

BACHI (ZAP)

EVANNA!!

E...

THOSE CREATURES WON'T BE BLINDED LONG, SO GET OUT OF THERE, AND QUICK!

GUEEE (GRAK!)

BUT HOW... WHAT... WHERE...?

LET'S TALK ABOUT IT LATER, ON DRY LAND.

HEE-HEE... I'M GLAD YOU THINK SO.

DELI-CIOUS!!

NO... BUT THANKS FOR THE THOUGHT.

I WISH THAT I COULD OBLIGE, BUT MY BLOOD WOULD POISON YOU.

LOOKS LIKE YOU HAVEN'T HAD ANY HUMAN BLOOD FOR QUITE A TIME.

BURU (SHIVER)

YOU DIDN'T NEED TO MENTION THAT PART...

AFTER WHAT WE'VE BEEN EATING FOR THE PAST MONTH, ANYTHING WOULD BE A GOURMET FEAST!!

MORE!

YOU'VE ALWAYS SAID YOU COULDN'T GET INVOLVED IN OUR BATTLES.

THEN WHY DID YOU RESCUE US?

A DIFFERENT ROUTE THAN YOU TOOK... BUT DON'T ASK ME TO EXPLAIN.

HOW DID YOU GET HERE?

THAT'S WHY I INTERVENED. AS PART OF YOUR QUEST, I CAN PLAY AN ACTIVE ROLE IN IT, AT LEAST FOR A WHILE.

I'M HERE TO ACT AS YOUR GUIDE ON THE NEXT STRETCH OF YOUR ADVENTURE.

NOT IN YOUR FIGHT WITH THE VAMPANEZE. WHEN IT COMES TO ALLIGATORS AND TOADS, I HAVE A FREE HAND.

...WE ARRIVED AT THE SHORES OF AN IMMENSE LAKE.

...AND THE SENTIENT BEINGS OF THIS PLANET HAVE YET TO DISCOVER IT.

I'M AFRAID IT IS NOT. IT'S A NEW FORMATION...

IS THIS THE LAKE OF SOULS?

I HAVE JUST THIS TO SAY, AND THEN I'LL DEPART...

AND NOW, I MUST LEAVE YOU.

YOU CAN'T TELL US...?

......

I'M SORRY.

IS THIS EARTH!?

YOU MEAN THERE ARE PEOPLE HERE? ARE THEY HUMANS?

THE SOUL OF THE PERSON HARKAT USED TO BE LIES WITHIN.

YOU MUST FISH FOR HIS SOUL...

THIS "LAKE OF SOULS" THAT YOU SEEK...

...HOUSES MANY TRAPPED SOULS, PEOPLE WHOSE SPIRITS DID NOT LEAVE EARTH WHEN THEY DIED.

IF YOU SUCCEED AND HARKAT LEARNS AND ACKNOWLEDGES THE TRUTH ABOUT HIMSELF, YOU WILL BE GUIDED HOME.

A NET USED TO TRAWL FOR THE DEAD...

YES, AND YOU'LL NEED A SPECIAL NET TO DO IT.

FISH IT? HIS SOUL!?

GRO-TESQUE...?

HOLY... LIQUID?

...YOU'LL NEED THE HOLY LIQUID FROM THE TEMPLE OF THE GROTESQUE.

AND TO ACCESS THE LAKE...

I THOUGHT SHE SAID NONE OF THE...PEOPLE HERE HAD FOUND THIS LAKE.

A BOAT! HOW DID SHE...?

AND YOU STILL HAVE THE PANTHER'S FANGS? VERY GOOD.

TREAT THOSE GELATINOUS GLOBES KINDLY. BE CERTAIN THEY DO NOT SPLIT.

YOU WILL NEED TO TAKE THIS BOAT TO REACH THE TEMPLE OF THE GROTESQUE ON THE FAR SHORE.

EVANNA ...?

HYUUUU (WHOOOSH)

72

I'LL BE OVER-JOYED TO SEE LAND AGAIN...

HOW WIDE IS THIS DAMN LAKE?

WE ROWED THE LITTLE BOAT FOR FOUR WHOLE DAYS...

GII (CREAK)

GII

WHOA, WHAT'S HAPPENING!?

WHEW...

TAKE A BREAK, DARREN. THE LACK OF BLOOD IS WEARING ON YOU, ISN'T IT?

I'VE DEALT WITH FAR WORSE...

DON'T WORRY ABOUT ME.

IT'S COMING CLOSER...

WHAT SOUND?

THAT SOUND...

ZAPA (SPLASH)

NOTHING'S EVER CAUSED WAVES LIKE THIS BEFORE!

BO
(WHOOOSH)

YOUR NIGHT-MARES? NO, HARKAT!

I'VE SEEN THIS BEFORE... IN MY NIGHT-MARES...

...IT'S A DRAGON!

...BUT WE'RE FAR FROM THROUGH, DARREN...

CREPSLEY MIGHT BE DEAD...

IT'S THERE THAT I'LL PLUNGE YOU INTO A DEEPER HELL THAN YOU'VE EVER KNOWN.

...A SUITABLE STAGE FOR A FINAL CONFRON-TATION.

THE WAR OF THE SCARS NEEDS...

...CAN YOU?

OH, BUT I CAN'T WAIT... DARREN...

BASA (FLAP)

CHAPTER 89: THE LEGENDARY BEAST

CHAPTER 89:
THE LEGENDARY BEAST

LOOK OUT, IT'S COMING BACK AROUND !!

GOSHA CRUNCH

WE'RE DONE FOR! THERE'S NO ESCAPE !!

BUO

BUO (WHOOSH)

SUUUU (SHHHP)

DIVE, HARKAT! AS DEEP AS YOU CAN GO!!

BO (BWOOOF)

OH, HELL!!

FORGET IT! JUST GO!!

LAND!?

WE'RE ALMOST TO THE OTHER SIDE OF THE LAKE!

IS HE GOING BACK AFTER HARKAT AGAIN!?

PUHA (GASP)

STOP!! LEAVE HIM ALONE!!!

PIKU (TWITCH)

LET ME GO...

...YOU SON OF A—

WHA...?

82

BASHA
(SPLASH)

EASY, YOUNG 'UN!

YE AWAKE, THEN?

!!?

WHERE ...?

OI, HAR-KAT!

YER WEE FRIEND'S AWAKE!

HAR-KAT! SO ARE YOU!

DARREN, YOU'RE ALL RIGHT!

BA (WHAM)

TWO DAYS?

OF COURSE I AM! YOU'VE BEEN OUT FOR... ALMOST TWO DAYS!

SPITS ABRAMS. PLEASED T' MEET YE!

SPITS RESCUED US FROM THE LAKE.

Y-YOU'RE A FISHER-MAN?

KYORO (ROLL)

GYORO (ROLL)

I JEST FISHED YE OUT, SAME AS ANY FISHERMAN WOULD'VE!

BUN (SHAKE)

BUN

MANY THANKS, MR. ABRAMS.

WOW! SO THE GLOBES AND THE PANTHER FANGS ALL MADE IT OK?

PACHI

PACHI (POP)

SOMEHOW... MIRACULOUSLY.

...BUT THAT'S A LONG STORY. HOW ABOUT A BITE O' FOOD OUTSIDE?

I USED T' BE A PIRATE 'FORE I ENDED UP HERE...

DARREN'S CLOTHES ARE DRY AND REPAIRED.

ARE WE READY OUT THERE, HARKAT?

AND HAVE SOME POTEEN TO WASH IT DOWN! 'TWILL PUT HAIRS ON YER CHEST!

HEE HEE!

EAT UP, LAD! CAUGHT THE FISH MESELF!

YOU'RE FROM IRELAND?

GUBI (GLUG)

ME GRANDFATHER CAME FROM IRELAND AND HE TAUGHT ME ALL HIS BREWIN' SECRETS.

BREWED IT ALL MESELF FROM POTATOES.

I PREFER WHISKEY, BUT I HAS T' MAKE DO.

POTEEN?

HIKKU (CHIC)

OOF!

SPITS HAD BEEN A PIRATE IN THE FAR EAST IN THE 1930s.

HE RODE ON THE PRINCE OF PARIAHS, A SMALL, SPEEDY SHIP.

SO YOU CAME TO THIS PLACE FROM SOME-WHERE ELSE TOO!

SFX: GUBI

I S'POSE I'LL GIVE YE THE QUICK VERSION...

BUT IT WASN'T TO RESCUE THEM FROM DROWN-ING.

IT WAS BECAUSE MOST WHO JUMPED TO GET AWAY FROM THE PIRATES WERE TRYING TO SWIM FOR FREEDOM WITH THEIR JEWELS AND TREASURE INTACT!

IT WAS SPITS'S JOB TO FISH PEOPLE WHO JUMPED OVER-BOARD OUT OF THE SEA.

AND IT WAS THERE THAT HE MET ...

THE NEXT THING HE KNEW, HE WAS CLIMBING ONTO THE SHORE OF THIS VERY LAKE.

AS THE SHIP BROKE APART, SPITS JUMPED OVER-BOARD.

GOOO CWHOOSH

ONE NIGHT, THE PRINCE OF PARIAHS FOUND ITSELF AT THE CENTER OF A FIERCE STORM.

MR. TINY!!

THIS SMALL MAN IN BIG YELLOW GALOSHES.

HE HAD A GREAT FUNNY CLOCK IN HIS HANDS, IN THE SHAPE OF A HEART...

SFX: HIKKU (HUC)

HE TOLD ME I'D COME TO A PLACE FAR FROM THE ONE I KNEW, AND I WAS STUCK.

HE SAID THIS WAS A LAND O' DRAGONS.

AWFUL DANGEROUS FER HUMANS, BUT THERE WAS A SHACK WHERE I'D BE SAFE.

...AND THEY WOULD MAKE MY DREAMS COME TRUE!

...TWO PEOPLE WOULD COME ALONG EVENTU-ALLY...

IF I STAYED THERE AND KEPT A WATCH ON THE LAKE...

88

...AND I BEEN WAITING EVER SINCE, FIVE 'R SIX YEARS NEAR AS I CAN FIGURE.

PUHA (PWAA)

SO I SAT BACK, FISHED, FOUND SPUDS GROWING NEARBY, AND BROUGHT SOME BACK FER ME GARDEN...

YE WOULDN'T LEAVE OL' SPITS BEHIND!

HEE HEE HEE!

HUH?

YE'LL TAKE ME ALONG, WON'T YE?

OH, HARKAT TOLD ME ABOUT YER JOURNEY! GOING T' THE TEMPLE OF THE GROTESQUE, EH?

ACTUALLY, WE'RE ALSO ON A QUEST TO RETURN HOME...

SO TAKE ME BACK HOME, WON'T YE?

DON'T KNOW NOWT O' THE AREA.

NOPE. WITH ALL THE DRAGONS AROUND, I DON'T VENTURE FAR FROM THE SHED...

DO YOU KNOW WHERE TO FIND THE TEMPLE?

ZURURU (DRAG)

THIS IS ME TRUSTY NET. SLIPPED THROUGH WITH ME.

RIGHT-O!

PAN (SMACK)

SHOW DARREN THE NET.

HOW MANY TIMES DID I TELL YE? HEE! HEE HEE!

C-COME NOW, HAR-KAT!

HAS TO BE. THE NET THAT WAS USED... TO FISH FOR THE DEAD.

THINK THIS IS THE NET EVANNA SAID WE NEED?

SO I GUESS IT PROB-ABLY *HAS* DRAGGED UP CORPSES... ACCIDEN-TALLY, LIKE.

GYORO GYORO

GURU GSPIN

COURSE I NEVER FISHED FOR THE DEAD! MIND, I RECALL A COUPLE O' PEOPLE WHO DROWNED WHEN I WAS FISHING 'EM OUT.

NO PROOF THE TEMPLE WILL BE THERE... BUT I HAVE A FEELING ABOUT IT.

APPARENTLY THE DRAGONS FLY TO THE LAKE FROM THE SOUTH-EAST.

WHY SOUTH-EAST?

USE THE DARKNESS AND HEAD SOUTH-EAST T' AVOID THE DRAGONS!

IF YE WANT T' LEAVE FER THIS TEMPLE O' THE GROTESQUE, WE SHOULD LEAVE AT NIGHT!

HEE HEE! THE ADVEN-TURE OF OUR LIVES.

OOOH, I CAN HARDLY WAIT...

...THE WAY HIS EYES FLICK LEFT OR RIGHT WHEN HE'S LYING.

HE MAKES ME FEEL UNEASY...

...AND THERE MUST BE A REASON WHY... MR. TINY BROUGHT HIM HERE.

BUT HE'S GOT THE NET...

I NOTICED THAT TOO...

...CAN WE REALLY TRUST HIM?

SAY, HARKAT. I REALIZE HE'S HELPING US OUT, BUT...

BUT I DON'T LIKE TO DO IT SECRETLY...

PLUS, YOU NEED BLOOD SOON, DARREN. WHY NOT TAKE SOME OF HIS?

IF HE FINDS OUT YOU'RE A VAMPIRE... HE COULD TRY TO ATTACK YOU.

HE THINKS I'M A DEMON.

SPITS IS SUPERSTITIOUS.

UGH, THE STENCH...

HE DRINKS SO MUCH...

I NEED BLOOD, AND WE NEED THE NET...

...SO IT LOOKS LIKE WE DON'T HAVE MUCH CHOICE BUT TO TRAVEL WITH HIM.

YES, THANK-FULLY.

BETTER?

I'VE HAD ENOUGH O' THIS FILTHY POTEEN!!

BRING ME SOME BLASTED WHISKEY!!

BUT THAT DOESN'T MEAN...

...I FEEL LIKE I CAN TRUST HIM...

GORON (ROLL)

MM. MM. MM.

OOH HEE

HEE HEE HEE

YE DON'T SCARE SPITS ABRAMS !!!

GI' ME YER WORST, YE GREAT UGLY BEASTS!!

HEE HEE!

STOP THAT, SPITS! GET IN THE SHADOWS!

CHAPTER 90: GROTESQUE

SAID I WAS A MONSTER! NOT FIT T' SHARE A SHIP WITH 'EM! BUT I'LL SHOW 'EM!!

THEY THINK THEY WAS SO HIGH AND MIGHTY! BETTER THAN DUMB OLD SPITS!

URRP... HIC!

JUST PUT THE KNIFE AWAY!

OKAY, SPITS! ALL RIGHT!

GOT TO GO BAIL OUT THE BILGE WATER!

JEST A MINUTE...

DARREN! OVER THIS WAY!

BY THE TIME THE MOON ABOVE HAD SHARPENED INTO A SLIVER...

LOOKS LIKE TROUBLE!

KRP...!

YES! WE FINALLY MADE IT!!

...OF THE GROTESQUE!!

IT'S THE TEMPLE...

SOME PIRATE YOU MUST HAVE BEEN!

SCARED ALREADY, SPITS?

I DON'T LIKE THE LOOK O' THIS PLACE.

...AND I KNOWS WHAT IT REALLY IS—A TEMPLE O' DEATH!

AHH, BUT THAT'S HOW I KNOW. A PIRATE LEARNS T' SENSE DANGER...

SFX: KACHI (RATTLE) KACHI

I HEAR... HUMAN VOICES?

WHAT IS IT, DARREN?

BUT THIS COULD BE THE PLACE WHERE WE FIND A CLUE TO RETURNING HOME...

IT'S EVEN MORE IMPOSING UP CLOSE...

ARE THEY THE "PEOPLE" OF THIS WORLD?

BROWN SKIN...PINK HAIR? AND WHITE EYES...

WHAT ARE THEY DOING? I'VE NEVER HEARD THIS LANGUAGE BEFORE.

KULASHKA!!

KULASHKA!!

ZURU
(SLIDE)

KU...
LASHKA?
WHAT
DOES IT
MEAN?

THEY'RE
JUST
CHANTING
THAT WORD,
OVER AND
OVER...

L-LOOK!
SOME-
THING'S
COMIN'
OUT O' THE
TEMPLE!

KULASHKA!!

KULASHKA!!

HITA
(SPLAT)

SAINTS
O' THE
SAILORS
!!

KA
(THUK)

WHAT IS HE
DOING!?

I
SEE
IT...

HAR-
KAT.

ZUZU
(ZRRD)

I
HAVE A
FEELING
...

...THAT'S
WHAT
EVANNA
WAS
TALKING
ABOUT
...

GOPO
(BLORP)

THE "HOLY LIQUID."

...BUT NOT THAT. IT WAS A TRUE MONSTER...

I THOUGHT I WAS PREPARED FOR ANY- THING...

THE MONSTER WILL HAVE YE BOTH FOR PUDDING!

KEE HEE HEE! ARE YE MAD?

HUH !?

...WE DON'T HAVE ANY CHOICE BUT TO GO AFTER IT...

STILL ...

AND A SNAKE NORMALLY SLEEPS... WHILE IT'S DIGESTING. THIS COULD BE OUR CHANCE...

A MAN WOULD TAKE A LONG TIME TO DIGEST, EVEN FOR A BEAST OF THAT SIZE.

I'M NOT SURE ABOUT THAT. IT FED LIKE A SNAKE.

THEY'RE COMING OUT OF THE TEMPLE!

SHH!

ARRR! KEE HEE HEE!

AND IT LOOKS IT!

"GRO-TESQUE."

BUT THIS AIN'T A SNAKE. IT'S A... WHAT DID YE CALL IT?

ZORO

ZORO (TROMP)

HARKAT ...

SHOULD WE TRY... TALKING TO THEM? MAYBE THEY'LL ...

THEY MUST BE KEEPING IT INSIDE THE TEMPLE.

I DIDN'T SEE ANYONE CARRYING THE VIAL.

WE'LL BE BACK.

I'LL WAIT OUT HERE.

WELL, I AIN'T GONNA CHUCK MY LIFE AWAY ON A CRAZY THING LIKE THIS!

WILL WE EVEN UNDERSTAND EACH OTHER?

THERE'S NO WAY THEY'LL BELIEVE OUR STORY.

GOOD POINT... SORRY.

I'LL CARRY AHEAD AND LOOK FER YER LAKE O' SOULS MYSELF...

KACHI
(CRATTLE)

IF IT HOLDS THE DEAD LIKE YE SAY, I MIGHT MEET YE THERE!

WELL, AT LEAST THE COAST IS CLEAR...

LOOK UP, DARREN...

THERE IT IS... FAST ASLEEP.

BUT WHERE'S THE HOLY LIQUID...?

SFX: GUBUBU (BLUB)

WOW, WHAT A PLACE TO PUT IT...

THERE.

CAREFUL NOW...

HOP UP...

SFX: GOPO (BLURP)

BETTER TAKE A FEW MORE, JUST IN CASE...

SO THE "HOLY LIQUID" IS A POISON TAKEN FROM THE MONSTER'S FANGS...

I ASSUME IT'S SOME... KIND OF POISON.

WELL, IT WAS COLLECTED FROM THE GRO-TESQUE'S FANGS.

WHAT IS THIS STUFF, ANY-WAY?

LOOKS DEADLY TO THE TOUCH...

GUBUBU

HOW COULD SUCH A THING EXIST?

GUBUBU (BLUB)

IT WAS LIKE A BUNCH OF HUMAN BEINGS MUSHED INTO A PULP.

DOES THAT MEAN THIS WORLD OF DRAGONS ISN'T EARTH AFTER ALL?

AND THESE PEOPLE WORSHIPPING THE GROTESQUE AREN'T NORMAL BY OUR STANDARDS.

KULASHKA!!

KULASHKA!!

TA CHOP!

QUIET!!!

SHH!

FORGET IT! LET'S JUST GET OUT OF HERE!

WE'VE GOT TO STOP THEM BEFORE THEY CALL MORE!

BA (GRAB)

KULASHKA!!

KULASHKA!!

KULASHKA!!

BIHYU (SWISH)

BURURU (TREMBLE)

JUMP!!!

BA (LEAP)

CHAPTER 91: GETAWAY

DOSHA
(SLAM)

GAGO
(CRUNCH)

ROLL,
HAR-
KAT
!!

KORO
(ROLL)

KORO

GUGU
(TUG)

PORO
(SLIP)

ZASA
(SWISH)

JIRI
(GRIT)

YEAH...
THEY'RE
MAD.

I DON'T
UNDER-
STAND
THE LAN-
GUAGE...
BUT I
KNOW
WHAT
THEY'RE
SAYING.

ZUSA
(SLIDE)

Y-YOU
WANT
THE
VIAL!?

SU
(SWISH)

THEY'RE AFRAID... OF THE POISON!

IT'S EITHER REALLY SACRED... TO THEM, OR REALLY DANGEROUS.

ZA
(ZSHH)

I GUESS THEY WON'T LET US GO...FOR FREE.

HE WANTS US TO REPLACE THE VIALS FIRST.

THEY OPENED A PATH.

ARE THEY LETTING US PASS?

...

...I'LL NEVER SPEAK TO YOU AGAIN.

OKAY... BUT IF THEY KILL US ON THE WAY OUT...

WHAT? BUT WE NEED THE LIQUID FOR—

NO CHOICE... WE HAVE TO RETURN THEM.

NO USE IN KEEPING IT IF...WE END UP DEAD...

SFX: BURURU (BRRP)

FEAR NOT, LADS! THE FLEET'S HERE T' SAVE YE!!!

BOGOHH
(KABOOOM)

...IT'S LIQUID EXPLO-SIVE!!!

THE HOLY LIQUID ISN'T POISON...

AHH!

AHHHH!

IT EX-PLODED!!!!

NO TIME T' THINK! HOP IN, BOYS!

HEEHEE!

ZUZAZA (SLIDE)

THE EXPLOSION MUST HAVE CREATED THIS HOLE! IT'S DEEP!

WE'RE IN FER IT NOW! THE YAWNIN' GATES O' HELL AWAIT!

GOGOGO (CRUMBLE)

THERE'S NO OTHER WAY OUT!

GARA (CLUNK)

GAGOGO (CRUMBLE)

DA (DASH)

YOU GUYS GO AHEAD!!!

GAAN (CRUNCH)
ZUZUUN (GZMMM)

NNG...
URGH...

GOOD THING THERE'S A CAVE UNDER HERE...

LOOKS LIKE WE'RE UNDER THE TEMPLE.

WHERE ARE WE?

GU (SHOVE)

SOME-HOW...

HARKAT... SPITS... YOU GUYS ALIVE?

DOESN'T LOOK LIKE WE'RE GETTING OUT THIS WAY...

NOT BUDGING AN INCH.

WHEW

WE'D AGREED TO A DEAL... THEY WERE LETTING US GO!

WE WEREN'T THE ONES WHO... TOSSED BOMBS WHEN THERE WASN'T A NEED!

MU CHMPH
MOG...

TCH!

...WE'D HAVE ALL THE FRESH AIR IN THE WORLD T' BREATHE!

IF YE HADN'T GONE PRANCING ABOUT IN THAT BLOODY TEMPLE...

HAVE WE BEEN BURIED ALIVE, THEN?

WHAT'D YE SAY!?

WHAT'S IMPORTANT IS THAT WE HAVE THE HOLY LIQUID NOW.

LET'S CONCENTRATE ON FINDING A WAY OUT AND LEAVE THE FINGER-POINTING FOR ANOTHER TIME.

EASY, YOU TWO...

THEY'D'VE STRUNG YE UP AND HAD YE FER BREAKFAST!

BAH!

HMPH.

MIGHT AS WELL MOVE ONWARD AND HOPE FOR THE BEST.

IT LOOKS LIKE WE'VE GOT A TUNNEL TO FOLLOW NOW.

TOO HOT...

HUFF.

HUFF.

I CAN'T SEE. IT'S PITCH BLACK...

!?

COME ON, SPITS. IT'S ONLY BEEN THIRTY MINUTES.

CRAZY LANDLUBBERS... WHEN DO WE STOP WALKIN'?

HERE GOES NOTHING...

DON'T DO IT! YE DON'T KNOW WHAT'LL JUMP OUT!

LET'S OPEN IT.

WHAT... IS THIS THING?

WHA IS IT?

GAKON (THUNK)

BUT THERE'S NO OTHER PLACE TO GO...

DOOR?

IT'S LIKE A DOOR OR SOMETHING...

BUN (VMMM)

STILL DARK...

EEP!

CHIKA

JIJI

JI (ZZT)

CHIKA (FLICK)

JI

PA (FLICK)

EEEEE!!

THIS LOOKS LIKE...

OHH! LOOK AT THAT!

WHAT... IS THIS...?

...

WHISKEY! IT'S WHISKEY!!

IS THIS EVEN POSSIBLE...?

THIS CAN'T BE...

WAIT, SPITS!!

SOMETHIN' TOUCHE ME NECK!

KASASA (SCUTTLE)

KASA

AT A SPECIAL MOUNTAIN FAR FROM HERE. THEY SHOULDN'T BE FOUND IN A PLACE LIKE THIS...

YES, THEY LIVE AT VAM—

BA' SHAN? YE KNOW WHAT IT IS?

I CAN'T BELIEVE IT, BUT IT'S TRUE.

DARREN, THAT LOOKS LIKE...

A BA' SHAN'S SPIDER.

"THERE'S A SECRET EXIT TUNNEL BEHIND THE REFRIGERATOR.

"IT'S A FEW HUNDRED YARDS TO THE SURFACE.

"CONGRATULATIONS ON OVERCOMING THE OBSTACLES TO DATE.

"HERE'S HOPING ALL GOES WELL IN THE FINAL STRETCH. BEST REGARDS ...

"AFTER THAT, YOU FACE A SHORT WALK TO THE VALLEY WHEREIN LIES THE LAKE OF SOULS.

...ilations on to date. Here's hoping stretch. Best regards, and sincere benefactor —

Desmond Ti...

"...YOUR DEAR FRIEND AND SINCERE BENEFACTOR ...

"...DESMOND TINY."

THE FRIDGE, FOOD, AND DRINKS... ARE ALL FROM OUR WORLD.

I WONDER WHERE ALL THIS...CAME FROM!

IT WOULD EXPLAIN THE MESSAGE.

I'LL BET MR. TINY MUST HAVE TRANSPORTED ALL OF THIS HERE.

CHU (SMOOCH)

CHU

CHAPTER 92:
BOMB

KU-LASH... KAS?

IT MAKES MORE SENSE THAN SUGGESTING THE KULASHKAS BUILT THIS PLACE.

IT'S LIKE THEY WERE LEFT JUST FOR ME.

LOOK, THERE'S EVEN SOME PICKLED ONIONS.

THE PEOPLE UP THERE WHO WOR-SHIPPED THE GRO-TESQUE.

GOT TO CALL THEM SOMETHING, DON'T WE?

"KULASH-KAS"... YES, I SEE.

THEIR APPEAR-ANCE... AND THE WAY THEY TALKED!

AHA! I KNEW THEY REMINDED ME...OF SOMEONE!

...!

THEY WERE LIKE THE GUARDIANS OF THE BLOOD!

SFX: KASA (SCUTTLE)

...IT WOULD EXPLAIN WHY THERE ARE SO MANY HERE...

AND IF THE GUARDIANS OF THE BLOOD BROUGHT THESE BA'SHAN'S SPIDERS WITH THEM...

...IN ORDER FOR THEM TO BUILD THE TEMPLE OF THE GROTESQUE...

BUT IF MR. TINY TRANS-PORTED THEM HERE, JUST LIKE THIS KITCHEN...

IT'S NOT OUT OF THE QUES-TION.

...THEN THE CHANGES MIGHT BE DUE TO THEIR EVOLVING TO SUIT THE ENVIRON-MENT.

TRUE, THERE WERE SIMILARITIES, BUT THEY WERE DIFFERENT. THEIR EYES WERE DULL...

...AND THE HAIR WAS PINK...

REMEMBER, SPITS WAS BROUGHT HERE TO THIS WORLD...

...BY MR. TINY, JUST LIKE THE KITCHEN AND SPIDERS.

WHAT FOR?

IF THAT'S THE CASE, THEN WE SHOULD BE GRATEFUL TO SPITS.

HEE HEE!

...AND MOST OF ALL, WE NEED HIM TO FISH THE SOUL FROM YOUR PREVIOUS LIFE OUT OF THE LAKE...

...AND WE WOULDN'T KNOW THE HOLY LIQUID IS EXPLOSIVE IF HE HADN'T BARGED INTO THE TEMPLE...

WITHOUT HIM, I WOULDN'T HAVE ANY BLOOD...

I HOPE THIS IS THE LAST TIME I NEED TO TAKE HIS BLOOD IN SECRET...

GOKU (GULP)

PACHI (CLICK)

NOW LET'S GET SOME REST BEFORE WE HEAD OUT...

I THINK WE'RE FINALLY GETTING TO THE END OF MR. TINY'S COMPLEX LITTLE RIDDLE.

WE'LL HAVE OUR ANSWERS VERY SOON.

THE LAKE OF SOULS...

YE SAID IT, DEMON...

GEE HEE HEE...

BUT HOW WILL WE GET UP CLOSE TO IT...?

......

SO THIS IS WHERE WE'LL FISH FOR THE SOUL OF HARKAT'S PAST LIFE...

IT'S A NEST O' DRAGONS. THEY GUARD THE LAKE.

THE BIGGEST DRAGON DOWN THERE IS THE ONE THAT ATTACKED US.

YE NEVER ASKED, DID YE?

DON'T YOU THINK WE'D HAVE WANTED... TO KNOW ABOUT THAT?

HEE HEE!

JEST LIKE THAT MR. TINY SAID.

AND EVEN IF WE DO, WE'LL HAVE NO TIME TO CAST OUR NET.

IT'LL BE IMPOSSIBLE TO REACH THE LAKE AND AVOID FIVE SETS OF EYES.

THE TWO SMALL ONES ARE CLEARLY INFANTS, WHILE THE TWO MEDIUM-SIZED ONES MUST BE FEMALES.

KUEEE (KRAWW)

IT LOOKS LIKE THE BOSS OF THE GROUP...

DON'T YE WORRY ABOUT WHAT T' DO WHEN WE GETS THERE.

GUE (GRAW)

GUE (GRAW)

SEE WHERE THERE'S NOWT A BLADE O' GRASS AROUND THE WATER'S EDGE?

IF YE GET THAT CLOSE T' THE LAKE, THE DRAGONS CAN'T HARM YE...

AND I AIN'T OF NO MIND T' FALL IN MESELF...

HEE HEE!

UNLESS A LIVING PERSON JUMPS OR FALLS IN, THE DRAGONS CAN'T COME NEAR.

AYE, THERE'S A SPELL ON THE LAKE.

MR. TINY TOLD YOU THAT TOO?

IS IT GOING OFF TO HUNT?

LOOKS LIKE THE LAKE IS NEVER... WITHOUT A DRAGON GUARDING IT.

THE MALE GOES TO FIND FOOD...AND LEAVES THE FEMALES AND BABIES BEHIND.

BASA-CFLAP!

HYUUU CWHOOSH!

WELL, THAT SOLVES THE ISSUE OF WHAT TO DO AFTER WE GET TO THE EDGE OF THE LAKE...

...BUT STILL, HOW TO APPROACH IT?

LOOK, DARREN.

BOMBS?

'TIS A PITY BOOM BOOM BILLY AIN'T WITH US. HE WAS A WONDER WITH BOMBS...

NO, SPITS. WE'RE TRYING TO DRIVE THEM OFF, NOT KILL THEM!

WE OUGHT T' BLAST THE BEASTS WITH THE VIAL, LIKE THAT GROTESQUE!

THAT'S IT! BOMBS!

CAP'N SAID BILLY WAS WORTH HIS WEIGHT IN GOLD...

THAT'S WHAT ALL OF THIS WAS FOR!!

BA (SNATCH)

YOU HAVE AN IDEA?

BUT WE HAVE TO BE CARE-FUL NOT TO BREAK THE GLOBES, OR THE LIQUID MIGHT EXPLODE.

IN-JECT...?

BUT IF WE COULD SOMEHOW INJECT THE LIQUID INTO THE GLOBES, WOULDN'T THEY BE LIKE LITTLE BOMBS?

BY THEM-SELVES, THE GELATINOUS GLOBES AND HOLY LIQUID ARE WORTH-LESS...

AH!

THERE'S ONE MISSING STEP...

THAT'S IT!

THE HOLLOW PANTHER'S TOOTH...

WHAT ABOUT THIS... DARREN?

GOSO
(RUSTLE)

FFF...

FFF...

IF THIS BLOWS UP IN MY FACE...

TORO
(DRIP)

ト口...

ズ
(SHHP)

...I'M DEAD MEAT.

JIWA
(GEEP)

ジワ...

CARE-FUL, DAR-REN.

OOH...

HERE WE GO! ONE HOLY GELATINOUS BOMB, READY TO GO!!

PURU (JIGGLE)

FUUU (FWOO)

WHAT ABOUT ME!?

I'LL TAKE HALF OF THE BOMBS, AND HAR-KAT GETS THE OTHER HALF.

AND THE VIAL IS EMPTY.

JUST ENOUGH TO FILL ALL THE GLOBES WE HAD.

WE DON'T WANT SPITS TRYING TO KILL THOSE DRAGONS...

WELL, IF YE SAY SO...

......

WE NEED YOU TO CONCENTRATE ON FISHING OUT HARKAT'S SOUL WITH YOUR NET, SPITS.

BUTSU (MUTTER)

BUTSU

HE NEVER LET SPITS TOUCH HIS PRECIOUS BOMBS EITHER...

JUST LIKE BOOM BOOM BILLY...

I CAN HARDLY WAIT FER IT!

AHH! AYE! OUR WORLD!

...?

ARRR... OUR WORLD?

ONCE WE GET THIS DONE, WE CAN RETURN TO OUR WORLD. ARE YOU EXCITED?

DOWN THE HATCH !!

BA (SWISH)

AND ONCE I'M BACK, I'M GONNA DRINK ME ALL THE WHISKEY THERE IS!

NO WAY. WE'RE TOO FAR AWAY FOR THEM TO—

I HOPE THAT BLAST DIDN'T ATTRACT THE... DRAGONS' ATTEN-TION.

EVERY-ONE OKAY!?

SHUUU (HISS!)

HEE HEE... NEARLY BLEW ME OWN HEAD OFF...

BASA

BASA (FLAP)

GOFUAA (FWOO)

NEVER MIND !!

GYAAAA (GRAWR)

BOGOO
(FLOOOM)

JUST MAKE A BREAK FOR THE EDGE OF THE LAKE!

SO MUCH FOR ALL OF OUR PLANNING!!

YEOWWW!!

ZASA
(SLIDE)

ZU
(SLIDE)

I REALLY HOPE THIS WORKS...

HERE COMES THE DRAGON!

DRIVE IT OFF!!

BUT HOW!?

GUGYAAA
(GRAWWK)

I'LL HANDLE HER!

HERE COMES ANOTHER ONE, HARKAT!

THE DRAGON'S KEEPING ITS DISTANCE...

HOO-HOOO! IT'S LIKE BOOM BOOM BILLY ALL OVER AGAIN!!

THESE BOMBS ARE REALLY DOING... THE TRICK, DARREN!!

LIKE I SAID, CAP'N ALWAYS CLAIMED BILLY WAS WORTH HIS WEIGHT IN GOLD!

HA-HA! SPITS SEEMS TO BE GETTING INTO THE SPIRIT OF THE ADVENTURE!

BOOM, BOOM, KABOOM! HEE HEEE!!

HYA! HYA!

HYA! HYA!

THAT'S WHY I CUT OFF BILLY'S ARM AND DEMANDED GOLD FOR IT!!

DONN (BOOM)

BO (BOOM)

GO (BOOM)

WE'RE TOO CLOSE TO PULL BACK NOW! JUST HAVE TO REACH THE LAKE!

WE'RE DOWN TO ABOUT... HALF OUR STOCK! WE DON'T HAVE ENOUGH TO MAKE IT BACK!

DOPA (BAKOOM)

¡GOPA (BOOM)

¡EEH!

GO (WHOOSH)

...AND MORE!!

IT'S BEAUTIFUL... ALL I EVER DREAMT...

OHH...

ARE WE WITHIN THE SAFE ZONE?

THE DRAGONS ARE KEEPING THEIR DISTANCE...

SO THIS...

THE SOULS OF THE DEAD... ...FLOATING BACK AND FORTH.

...IS THE LAKE OF SOULS!!

THEY JUST KEEP CIRCLING OVERHEAD.

SUPPOSEDLY THEY CAN'T TOUCH US IN THIS STRIP WITHOUT GRASS, AS LONG AS NO LIVING HUMAN FALLS INTO THE LAKE.

URO
(PEER)

URO

SPITS WAS RIGHT...

CHAPTER 93: SOULS

BASA
(FLAP)

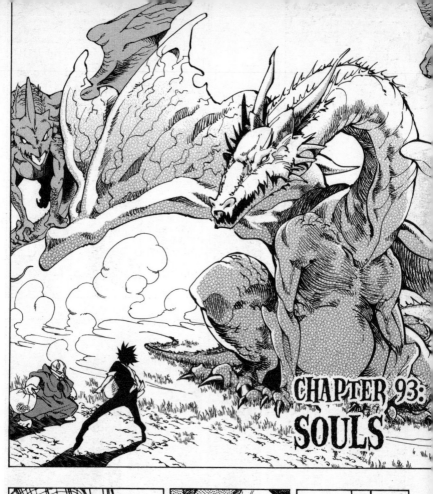

CHAPTER 93:
SOULS

BA
(WHOOSH)

EE
HEE
HEE
HEE!!

WE
NEED
TO FIND
YOUR
SOUL IN
HERE,
QUICK.

THE
MALE
DRAG-
ON IS
BACK.

HEE HEE! GOT ONE!

BUT ONCE YE HAUL 'EM UP ON LAND...

ALL ME DREAMS ARE COMING TRUE! HE WASN'T LYING!

THE LITTLE MAN TOLD ME 'TWOULD BE LIKE THIS, BUT I NEVER BELIEVED IT TILL NOW.

THESE SOULS MAY BE NOWT BUT GHOSTIES IN THE WATER...

GEEHEEHEE!

DREAMS?

!!

GU (GRAB)

LET GO OF THE NET!!

WAIT, NO! STOP IT, SPITS!

ALL WE NEEDED YOU TO DO WAS FISH THE SOUL OUT OF THE WATER!!

MURLOUGH ISN'T YOUR PAST LIFE, IS HE, HARKAT...?

WAS THAT... MURLOUGH!?

...THAT WAS MURLOUGH AS HE WAS IN LIFE!

THAT WASN'T A SOUL...

I JUST PULLED THE FREAK OUT O' THE WATER!

PAST LIFE!? THE HELL YE SAY!

ENOUGH O' THE GAMES, OR I'LL SKIN YE ALIVE!

LOOK WHAT YE DID, LAD! HE GOT AWAY!

JUST AS THEY WAS BEFORE THEY DIED!!

HEE-HEE! THAT'S HOW IT WORKS, LAD! ONCE YE FISH THEM OUT, THEY COME T' LIFE IN THEIR OLD BODIES!

...AN IMP AND A BLOOD-SUCKER!!

HYA HYA!

AND NOW I'M FINALLY DONE WITH THE LIKES OF YE...

YE INTERRUPTED ME LAST HAUL, BUT I'LL BRING 'EM ALL BACK!!

AND NOW NOBODY CAN STOP ME!

YE FED FROM ME WHEN YE THOUGHT I WAS ASLEEP!

GEE-HEE-HEE! YE THOUGHT I DIDN'T KNOW WHAT YE WAS, BUT SPITS AIN'T AS DUMB AS HE LETS ON.

KILL 'N' HAUL, KILL 'N' HAUL...

WHEN YE KILL THE SOUL, IT GOES BACK INTO THE WATER!

HEE HEE... IT'S A LAKE O' ENDLESS TREASURE...

KEE HEE!

I THOUGHT YOU SAID YOUR SHIP WAS... WRECKED IN THE NIGHT DURING A STORM...

THEY GRABBED ME IN THE MIDDLE O' THE NIGHT AND TOSSED ME RIGHT OVERBOARD!

ARRR... IT AIN'T TRUE!!

THEY'LL PAY FOR WHAT THEY DID T' POOR OL' SPITS!

NOW I CAN BRING BACK THE SOULS O' THE CAP'N AND THE OTHERS AND KILL 'EM AGAIN!

DEEP DOWN, THEY KNEW WHAT I WAS DOING AND ACCEPTED IT... BUT THEN THEY REPENTED AND CALLED ME A DEVIL! HYPOCRITES!!

WHAT WAS WRONG WITH KILLING AND EATING THE FOOLS I HAULED IN MY NETS? THE CREW GOT THEIR TREASURE, AND I GOT TO FEAST! IT WAS A FAIR DEAL!

GASHA (CRASH)

DAMN YE, DEMONS O' THE DARK! DAMN YE BOTH T' HELL!

THIS IS MAD-NESS, SPITS!

TO KILL AND EAT THE PEOPLE WHO TURNED ON YOU?

SO IT'S RE-VENGE YOU WANT ...

SFX: GASA (RUSTLE)

BUT YE DON'T GET T' KEEP SPITS FROM THIS ONE...

ARRR, BUT I KNEW YE WERE JUST LIKE THE FOOLS ON THE *PRINCE OF PARIAHS*...

DON'T DO IT, SPITS! WE DON'T WANT TO HURT YOU!

LET'S JUST GO BACK TO OUR WORLD, OKAY?

HYU (SWISH)

BYU (SLICE)

GARA (CLLINK)

GASHA

GI (GRK)

ZUSHA (SLIP)

GARA (STRIP)

NEVER! THIS IS MY DREAM!!

I'M RIGHT HERE IN PARADISE!!

BEHIND YOU...

S-SPITS...

ARR?

YE'D NEVER BETRAY OL' SPITS...

HEE HEE... AH, MY DEAR WHISKEY...

YER THE ONLY ONE THAT NEVER TURNED ON ME...

DIDN'T I TELL YE THEY COULDN'T COME NEXT NOR NEAR US AS LONG AS WE STAYED—

WHAT ARE YE UP TO NOW?

SFX: CHIRA (PEEK)

!!

BOU (BWOOF)

ARRR...

(JIRI) (TWINGE)

COME BACK, SPITS !!

GOO
(FWOOSH)

ZAPA
(SPLOOSH)

YORO
(WOBBLE)

...BUT I
WISH IT
COULD
HAVE
HAPPENED...
SOME
OTHER
WAY...

THE
CRAZY
CANNIBAL...
PROBABLY
DESERVED
IT...

THAT
WAS
AWFUL
...

OH
MAN...
POOR
SPITS
...

MERI...
(SQUISH)

DOSU
(THUDD)

GRRR
...

SPITS WAS STILL ALIVE WHEN HE...FELL INTO THE LAKE!!

UNLESS A LIVING PERSON JUMPS OR FALLS IN...

THE SPELL HAS BEEN BROKEN!!!

NO!!

BON (BOOM)

DAR-REN!!

I'LL DRAW THE DRAGON AWAY!

156

MY OWN... SOUL...?

GRAB THE NET AND FISH YOUR SOUL OUT!!

GU (GULP)

I CAN'T HOLD THE DRAGONS OFF MUCH LONGER!

ALMOST OUT OF BOMBS...

I GUESS I'LL HAVE TO GO FOR THE KILL!!

DOBON (KABOOM)

LEAVE ME ALONE!!!

GOS (THUD)

SOULS OF THE DEAD...I HAVE COME TO FIND MY OWN...

BUTSU (MUTTER)

BUTSU

SOULS OF THE DEAD, I CALL FORTH MY OWN...

ZUKI (THROB)

ZUKI

WHAT... WAS THAT !?

DO YOU HAVE IT, HARKAT !?

HERE GOES THE LAST ONE!

HURRY UP, HARKAT! WE'RE RUNNING OUT OF TIME!

BUTSU
BUTSU

THREE!

DOBO (KABOOM)

TWO!

I...

I HAVE IT!!!

GUI (TUG)

PULL!!

I CAN SEE IT! ALMOST THERE...

BUCHI (RIP)

BUCHI

BUTSU (POP)

I'LL HELP!!

IT'S... HEAVY!

GUGU (YANK)

THAT'S WHO I WAS IN MY PREVIOUS LIFE...

YES! WE'VE GOT HIM UP!

BASHA (SPLAASH)

!!!!!

HFF...

HFF...

WH... WHAT THE...?

YES... THAT'S ME...

I'M HIM...

UHH...

HARKAT!!

HARKAT! THAT CAN'T BE WHO YOU WERE!

!!

I WAS...

I AM...

161

I DIDN'T EXPECT IT TO GO THAT CLOSE TO THE WIRE!

IT'S LIKE THE DRAGON AND FLAME ARE... FROZEN IN MIDAIR...

I FEEL... NO HEAT...

AHH?

AHH... AH...

TIGHT TIMING, BOYS!

PACHI (CLAP)

PACHI

A THRILLING FINALE!

MOST SATIS-FYING ...!!!

KA (TOK)

KA

CHAPTER 94:
FATE

LET'S SEE, FIRE, FIRE... THIS SHOULD DO.

I'VE STOPPED TIME. IT WILL NOT RESUME UNTIL I SAY SO.

HAVE NO FEAR.

OOH!

BOWA (BWOOF)

NOW IF I SIMPLY TURN TIME BACK ON FOR THIS LICK OF FLAME...

AH, BUT DRAGON FIRE IS ALWAYS DIFFICULT TO CONTROL... WHEN WILL I LEARN?

HEE HEE!

IT'S ME...

NO...

I DON'T KNOW HOW... BUT IT IS.

WHAT'S GOING ON? HARKAT CAN'T HAVE BEEN KURDA!

HE WAS AROUND LONG BEFORE KURDA DIED!

DO YOU REMEMBER EVERYTHING THAT HAPPENED?

...SINCE I WAS PUT TO DEATH?

HOW MUCH TIME HAS PASSED...

SFX: BURU (SHIVER)

I'D RATHER NEVER THINK ABOUT THAT DROP INTO THE PIT OF STAKES AGAIN.

MY MEMORY'S AS SHARP AS EVER, THOUGH I WISH IT WASN'T.

I SEE... YOU HAVE MADE GREAT STRIDES ...

IS THAT ALL? LOOKING AT DARREN, I'D THOUGHT IT MUST BE LONGER...

EIGHT YEARS HAVE PASSED SINCE YOU DIED...

I'M STILL NOT A FULL VAMPIRE YET, THOUGH ...

I WENT THROUGH MY PURGE.

SO THE WAR OF THE SCARS HAS BEGUN...

...AND LARTEN IS NOW DEAD...

DO YOU DESPISE HIM FOR YOUR DEATH?

WHAT DO YOU THINK, KURDA? HERE IS DARREN, THE VERY MAN WHO FOILED YOUR PLANS...

I WAS CREATED YEARS BEFORE... KURDA DIED.

I KNOW I WAS KURDA. BUT *HOW?*

IT SEEMS YOU ARE RECOVER-ING THE MEMORIES OF YOUR TIME AS KURDA!

HE DID WHAT HE THOUGHT WAS BEST, AND FAILED... THAT'S ALL.

I DON'T... I MEAN, KURDA DOESN'T HATE DARREN.

UGH

SORRY... THIS IS CONFUS-ING...

THANK YOU, HAR-KAT...

... KEEPING THE WORLD ON A CHAOTIC KEEL.

BY PLAYING WITH TIME, I CAN SUBTLY INFLUENCE THE COURSE OF FUTURE EVENTS ...

IT'S MORE INTERESTING THAT WAY...

FROM THE PRESENT, I CAN MOVE BACKWARD INTO THE PAST OR FORWARD INTO ANY OF THE POSSIBLE FUTURES.

TIME IS RELATIVE.

TRAVEL THROUGH TIME IS MY ONE GREAT THRILL IN LIFE.

FOR REASONS OF MY OWN, I DECIDED TO MEDDLE WITH MASTER SHAN'S FATE!

I NEEDED A LITTLE PERSON WHO'D CARED ABOUT YOU WHEN HE WAS ALIVE, WHO'D DO THAT LITTLE BIT EXTRA TO PROTECT YOU.

SO I WENT INTO A POSSIBLE FUTURE, SEARCHED AMONG THE SOULS OF THE TORMENTED DEAD...

...AND FOUND OUR OLD FRIEND KURDA SMAHLT.

M-MY... FATE?

IN ORDER TO SAVE YOU. THINK UPON THE MANY TIMES THAT HARKAT HAS SAVED YOUR LIFE.

WELL, HARKAT HAS PERFORMED ADMIRABLY IN PROTECTING DARREN.

HE IS MOST DESERVING OF HIS REWARD.

I RETURNED TO THE TIME OF KURDA'S DEATH AND SWITCHED HIS CORPSE WITH ANOTHER'S.

I USED KURDA'S BONES TO MAKE HARKAT.

I WAS MADE...

...TO PROTECT DARREN.

HAS THERE EVER BEEN SUCH IRONY?

SO, IN EFFECT, AS HARKAT, I HELPED DARREN MASTERMIND MY OWN DOWNFALL!

PRECISELY! WITHOUT HARKAT, DARREN WOULD HAVE DIED LONG AGO, AND THE LORD OF THE VAMPANEZE WOULD SIMPLY HAVE LED HIS FORCES TO VICTORY OVER THE VAMPIRES.

SO YOU TOOK MY SOUL FROM THE FUTURE BACK TO THE PAST IN ORDER TO KEEP DARREN ALIVE...

I IDN'T... KNOW...

BUT I DIDN'T KNOW... THAT I USED TO BE KURDA...

YOU TOOK TO MY PLAN WITHOUT PROTEST.

YOU WERE UNABLE TO FORGIVE YOURSELF FOR BETRAYING YOUR PEOPLE, AND DESPERATE TO MAKE AMENDS.

YOUR SOUL WAS IN AGONY.

BUT ON A SUBCONSCIOUS LEVEL, YOU KNEW. THAT'S WHY YOU FOUGHT SO BRAVELY BESIDE DARREN.

IF YOU'D KNOWN WHO YOU WERE, IT WOULD HAVE CAUSED PROBLEMS.

SINCE I HAD TO RETURN YOUR SOUL TO THE PAST, I HAD TO HIDE THE TRUTH OF YOUR IDENTITY FROM YOU.

A SUBLIMELY PRISTINE CONCLUSION TO THIS TALE!

HARKAT HAS DONE WHAT HE NEEDED TO DO, ATONING FOR KURDA'S SINS AND BRINGING HIM BACK TO LIFE.

THIS WAS ONLY POSSIBLE THROUGH KURDA AND DARREN, A FRIENDSHIP THAT TRANSCENDS TIME!

HOW WILL WE BOTH EXIST...AT THE SAME TIME?

SO... DOES THIS MEAN THAT KURDA WILL RETURN TO OUR WORLD... WITH US?

NIYA (SMIRK)

SIMPLY TAKE A GOOD LOOK AT YOUR BODY, HARKAT.

I'M AFRAID YOU CAN'T— AT LEAST, NOT FOR VERY LONG.

WHAT ABOUT HAR-KAT?

WH-WHAT DO YOU MEAN?

WITHIN A DAY YOUR BODY WILL DISSOLVE, RELEASING YOUR SHARE OF THE SOUL.

THE STRANDS OF YOUR FORM ARE UNRAVELING.

WH... WHAT'S HAPPEN-ING...?

AS THE ORIGINAL, KURDA HAS A NATURAL CLAIM TO EXISTENCE. HARKAT'S HALF OF THE SOUL MUST DEPART THIS WORLD...

A SPLIT SOUL CAN NEVER BE REJOINED. HARKAT AND KURDA ARE TWO DIFFERENT PEOPLE.

PORO (DRIP)

PORO

PORO

NOW THAT KURDA'S SOUL HAS BEEN GIVEN FORM, THERE CAN ONLY BE ONE THAT EXISTS.

WHEN A LITTLE PERSON LEARNS OF HIS TRUE IDENTITY, IT BEGINS TO UNDO THE SPELL I CAST TO AFFIX THE SOUL TO HIS BODY.

STOP SPLITTING HAIRS! WHAT DO YOU MEAN!?

HEH! HE'S DEAD ALREADY.

YOU MEAN HARKAT'S GOING TO DIE!?

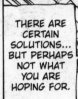

THERE ARE CERTAIN SOLUTIONS... BUT PERHAPS NOT WHAT YOU ARE HOPING FOR.

HEH HEH!

ANYTHING TO SAVE HARKAT!

ISN'T THERE ANYTHING WE CAN DO?

HE'S ONLY HERE BECAUSE YOU TOLD HIM THE NIGHTMARES WOULD KILL HIM OTHERWISE!!

DON'T GIVE ME THAT! HARKAT CAME ALL THIS WAY SO THAT HE COULD STAY ALIVE!

STOP IT, DARREN.

YOU SCHEMING RAT!

GA (GRAB)

HEH! HELL AWAITS HIM, WHETHER MOVING FORWARD OR TURNING BACK.

MIGHT AS WELL CHOOSE THE MORE PEACEFUL METHOD, DON'T YOU THINK?

IS THAT CORRECT?

PIKU (TWITCH)

...THEN I SHOULD BE ABLE TO ALLOW HARKAT TO CONTINUE LIVING BY RETURNING TO THE LAKE OF SOULS.

IF OUR TWO SOULS CANNOT CO-EXIST AT ONCE...

K-KURDA...

WHO WILL LIVE... AND WHO WILL DIE?

...

THE DECI-SION IS YOURS, KURDA...

FSU (SWISH)

ELSE I WOULD HAVE BROUGHT IT UP MYSELF.

I HAD A HUNCH THAT YOU WERE CLEVER ENOUGH TO FIGURE OUT THE CHOICE.

KURDA ...

NO WONDER I GOT THE FEELING THAT YOU AND I... WERE SIMILAR IN SOME WAY.

... AND I NEVER REALIZED IT.

HOW STRANGE, THAT YOU WERE ME ALL ALONG...

HAR-KAT...

NOW IT IS YOUR TURN TO LIVE, HARKAT.

I'VE HAD MY FILL OF LIFE...

PARADISE... YES, THAT WOULD HAVE BEEN NICE. I COULD SEE GAVNER, ARRA... EVEN LARTEN AGAIN.

BUT I DON'T HAVE THE RIGHT...

...WITH THE OPPORTUNITY TO DIE WITH HONOR AND TRAVEL TO PARADISE!

I JUST DON'T UNDERSTAND! YOU HAD ANOTHER CHANCE AT LIFE...

PICHA
(SPLISH)

FRIENDS WHO FOUGHT ALONG-SIDE ME...

THIS PLACE MAY BE HELL, BUT THERE ARE FRIENDS HERE...

SHURU (SLIP)

KURDA...

BIRI (RIP)

I AM EN-TRUST-ING MY LIFE TO YOU.

I AM NOT DYING TWICE...

TAKE CARE OF DARREN.

IT WAS MY FAULT YOU DIED...

KURDA... I NEVER HAD THE CHANCE TO APOL-OGIZE TO YOU.

OUR PEOPLE ARE IN YOUR HANDS, DARREN!

THERE IS NO NEED FOR YOU TO APOL-OGIZE TO ME, DARREN.

THE PATH YOU TREAD WILL HAVE A GREAT EFFECT ON THE FUTURE OF ALL VAMPIRES...

HELLO, DARREN. HELLO, HARKAT.

SO WHERE ARE WE?

MR. TINY'S GONE. HE WALKED THROUGH THE GATE WITH US, THOUGH...

OH, KURDA...

MY BODY'S AS SOLID AS EVER AGAIN.

I HAD A FEELING YOU WOULD BE VISITING US ABOUT NOW.

I'M DELIGHTED ABOUT YOUR SAFE RETURN.

MR. TALL!!

AS KURDA, YOU ALWAYS CALLED ME HIBERNIUS.

AH, YOUR MISSION WAS A SUCCESS.

HELLO... HIBERNIUS.

I HAVE YOUR TENT READY FOR YOU.

YOU MUST BE TIRED FROM YOUR JOURNEY. YOU'VE EARNED A GOOD REST.

HARKAT MULDS, AND...

... KURDA SMAHLT.

I WONDER HOW DEBBIE AND ALICE ARE DOING, AND THE STATE OF THE WAR...

I CAN'T BELIEVE WE WERE IN THAT STRANGE WORLD FOR THREE WHOLE MONTHS.

...AND WE NEVER NOTICED!

THE ANSWER WAS IN FRONT OF US ALL ALONG...

THEY SEEM NORMAL AT FIRST GLANCE... BUT LOOK AT THE POSTMARK.

I FOUND THEM IN THAT UNDER-GROUND KITCHEN.

THEY'RE NICE... BUT WHAT'S THE BIG DEAL?

CAN YOU TAKE A LOOK AT THESE POST-CARDS, DARREN?

WERE WE IN THE PAST, OR ON ANOTHER PLANET ENTIRELY?

THE SPIRITS, THE GROTESQUE, THE DRAGONS... IT WAS ALL LIKE A CRAZY DREAM.

POST-MARK?

HUH ...?

HARKAT... I DON'T THINK WE WERE IN THE PAST OR ON A DIFFERENT WORLD...

...

NO... THAT DATE CAN'T BE RIGHT.

THAT'S NOT FOR ANOTHER TWELVE YEARS.

YES... I HAD.

I HAD SEEN THAT PLACE BEFORE ...

GOKUN (GULP)

EXACTLY. AND THEY'RE ALL LIKE THAT...

IT WAS THE WORLD OF HARKAT'S NIGHTMARES, THE ONE THAT EVANNA SHOWED TO ME...

WHAT YOU SAW WAS A SHADE OF THE FUTURE, WHEN EITHER THE VAMPIRES OR THE VAMPANEZE HAVE TRIUMPHED.

HOW COULD I FORGET THAT BARREN LAND, ECHOING WITH THE SOUND OF WINGS FLAPPING?

THE LAKE OF SOULS · END

...WAS THE FU-TURE!

I THINK THAT BARREN ...

... MONSTER-FILLED WASTE-LAND...

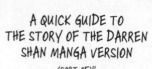

A QUICK GUIDE TO
THE STORY OF THE DARREN
SHAN MANGA VERSION
(SORT OF)!!

PART 10!!!!!!!!!

~TRIP TO ENGLAND: THE MOVING CONCLUSION~

WHY DID HE SPEAK TO ME IN JAPANESE?

THIS REALLY HAPPENED.

H-HUH? YOU SPEAK JAPANESE?

ER, I'M JAPANESE.

YOU KOREAN? CHINESE?

OH. SAYONARA.

I FEEL SO NERVOUS IN THIS FOREIGN COUNTRY...

IN FOGGY LONDON.

YOU. HEY, YOU.

...BUT I NEEDED TO GET SOMETHING OFF MY CHEST ABOUT MR. CREPSLEY'S DEATH.

I WAS ORIGINALLY GOING TO WRITE THIS UP FOR THE BONUS MATERIALS OF VOLUME 9...

I'M SORRY...

THIS IS THE CONTINUATION OF MY ENGLAND TRAVEL REPORT FROM VOLUME 8.

184

I HOPE TO DESCRIBE THE EXCITEMENT OF THIS ONE AT THE END OF VOLUME 11.

IT WAS MY FIRST TIME EVER CHEERING FROM THE STANDS FOR A MATCH!

ON THE SECOND DAY, I WENT TO THE STADIUM FOR CHELSEA, THE LOCAL SOCCER TEAM.

IT WAS LIKE BEING IN A FAIRY TALE! EVERYWHERE YOU LOOKED, IT WAS LIKE A LUSH PAINTING.

ON DAY 3, I VISITED THE COTSWOLDS FOR A BEAUTIFUL TRIP THROUGH TRADITIONAL ENGLISH SCENERY.

WHERE DO YOU THINK YOU'RE GOING?

...A SHORT, ELDERLY MAN WITH A WALKING STICK CALLED OUT TO ME.

WHO SAID ENGLISH FOOD IS TASTELESS!?

THE FISH AND CHIPS I HAD AT THE PUB THERE WAS THE BEST THING EVER!!

IT'S EVEN BETTER WITH VINEGAR!

HMM...

YOU THERE!!

ON THE WAY BACK, AS I WAS LOOKING FOR A BUS IN LONDON THAT WOULD TAKE ME TO MY HOTEL....

RANDOM GIRL WAITING AT THE BUS STOP

NOW HERE, LET ME TAKE A PICTURE FOR YOU! DON'T BE SHY, NOW!

YOU THERE, MISS, YOU TOO.

WE'RE ON THE WAY TO PICCADILLY CIRCUS.

WHAT? PICCADILLY CIRCUS!?

WELL, YOU WON'T GET THERE ON THIS BUS!

CERTAINLY NOT TO PICCADILLY CIRCUS!

SAY PICCADILLY!

KASHA (CLICK)

P...PICCADILLY...

EVERYONE IN ENGLAND WAS TERRIBLY NICE, AND I CANNOT COUNT THE NUMBER OF TIMES THAT I WAS HELPED BY A STRANGER.

AFTER THIS, THE OLD MAN VANISHED INTO THE LONDON NIGHT, LEAVING BEHIND ONLY THIS ONE STRANGE PHOTOGRAPH...

186

I ALSO WENT TO THE BRITISH MUSEUM, NATURAL HISTORY MUSEUM, AND EVEN A CASINO— IN SHORT, I HAD NEARLY ALL I COULD HANDLE OF LONDON.

...AND I GOT PLENTY OF PICTURES OF THE FAMOUS HAMPSTEAD NEIGHBORHOOD, POLICE STATIONS, AND HOSPITALS.

I WAS ALSO GIVEN A TOUR OF EAST LONDON, DARREN-SAN'S FAVORITE AREA...

BASHA (CLICK)

KASHA

KASHA

EUROPE'S TRAIN STATIONS HAVE A CHARM ALL THEIR OWN THAT IS QUITE DIFFERENT FROM JAPAN'S.

ON THE DAY I RELUCTANTLY LEFT THE CITY, I TRAVELED THROUGH TWO STATIONS BEFORE THE SUN HAD RISEN.

SO, WHAT ABOUT THAT CHAPTER?

AND THUS, MY NEARLY WEEK-LONG RESEARCH TRIP TO ENGLAND CAME TO A CLOSE.

GUOOO (SNORRR)

WE TOOK WELL OVER A THOUSAND PICTURES AND WALKED AT LEAST 100,000 STEPS ON OUR JOURNEY.

ONE LAST SECRET: I WAS HOPING TO DRAW UP A CHAPTER DRAFT ON THE FLIGHT, BUT I FELL ASLEEP ALL THE WAY TO OUR LANDING AT NARITA.

■ **The End** ■

MESSAGE FROM TAKAHIRO ARAI

WE'RE ALL FOUR-EYES!!!

I HAVE ENDLESS GRATITUDE FOR THE STAFF THAT PUTS TOGETHER SUCH INCREDIBLE WORK, WEEK IN AND WEEK OUT. A-KUN HAS BEEN THE BACKBONE OF MY OPERATION FROM THE VERY START, WITH HIS VERSATILITY IN ALL MATTERS FROM SCREENTONES TO BACKGROUNDS. T-KUN, THE NEW GUY, WHOSE EXCELLENT MANNERS AND WILL TO SUCCEED CONTINUE TO IMPROVE HIS GAME. AND MY BROTHER, JUNYA, WHOSE IMAGINATION HAS HELPED TO CRAFT THE LOOK OF THE *DARREN SHAN* MANGA WORLD BETTER THAN I EVER COULD. WHAT YOU SEE ON THESE PAGES IS CRAFTED FROM THE SWEAT AND BLOOD OF THESE THREE FINE GENTLEMEN.

THE SAGA OF DARREN SHAN ⑩

The Lake of Souls

Darren Shan
Takahiro Arai

Translation: Stephen Paul
Lettering: AndWorld Design
Art direction: Hitoshi SHIRAYAMA
Original cover design: Shigeru ANZAI + Bay Bridge Studio

Darren Shan Vol.10
Text © 2008 Darren Shan, Artworks © 2008 Takahiro ARAI
All rights reserved.
Original Japanese edition published in Japan in 2008 by Shogakukan Inc., Tokyo.
Artwork reproduction rights in the UK and The Commonwealth arranged with
Shogakukan Inc. through Tuttle-Mori Agency, Inc., Tokyo.

English translation © 2011 Darren Shan

Published in Great Britain by HarperCollins *Children's Books* in 2013
HarperCollins *Children's Books* is a division of HarperCollins*Publishers* Ltd,
77–85 Fulham Palace Road, Hammersmith, London, W6 8JB.

The HarperCollins website address is
www.harpercollins.co.uk

ISBN: 978-0-00-750644-6

Printed and bound in England by Clays Ltd, St Ives plc

MIX
Paper from
responsible sources
FSC www.fsc.org **FSC® C007454**

FSC™ is a non-profit international organisation established to promote the responsible
management of the world's forests. Products carrying the FSC label are independently
certified to assure consumers that they come from forests that are managed to meet
the social, economic and ecological needs of present and future generations, and other
controlled sources.

Find out more about HarperCollins and the environment at
www.harpercollins.co.uk/green